Seaside SANCTUARY

Seaside Sanctuary is published by Stone Arch Books
A Capstone Imprint
1710 Roe Crest Drive
North Mankato, Minnesota 56003
www.mycapstone.com

Library of Congress Cataloging-in-Publication Data
Names: Berne, Emma Carlson, author. | Madrid, Erwin, illustrator.
Title: The disappearing otters / by Emma Carlson Berne ; illustrated
  by Erwin Madrid.

Description: North Mankato, Minnesota : Stone Arch Books, [2019] |
  Series: Seaside Sanctuary | Summary: Elsa Roth is delighted with the
  sanctuary's five new river otters, but much less thrilled with the new
  volunteers, especially a sullen, troubled boy named Anson with a badly
  scarred face—and when the otters start going missing one of the other
  volunteers accuses him of stealing them, but Elsa is sure that he is not
  responsible, and she is determined to clear him and find the real thief.

Identifiers: LCCN 2018037069 | ISBN 9781496578600 (hardcover) | ISBN
9781496580290 (pbk.) | ISBN 9781496578648 (ebook pdf)
Subjects: LCSH: Otters—Juvenile fiction. | Marine parks and reserves—
  Juvenile fiction. | Wild animal trade—Juvenile fiction. | Theft—Juvenile
  fiction. | Malicious accusation—Juvenile fiction. | Friendship—Juvenile
  fiction. | CYAC: Otters—Fiction. | Marine parks and reserves—Fiction. |
  Wild animal trade—Fiction. | Stealing—Fiction. | Friendship—Fiction.
Classification: LCC PZ7.B455139 Di 2019 | DDC 813.6 [Fic]—dc23
LC record available at https://lccn.loc.gov/2018037069

Designer: Aruna Rangarajan
Photo Credits: Shutterstock: Color Brush, design element throughout, Crazy
nook, (otter) 108, KRAUCHANKA HENADZ, design element throughout,
Nikiparonak, design element throughout, Theeradech Sanin, design
element throughout

The author is grateful to Dr. Jeff Black, professor of wildlife at Humboldt
State University, for his introduction to the world of river otters and the
black-market exotic animal trade.

Printed in the United States of America.
PA49

The Disappearing Otters

by Emma Carlson Berne

illustrated by Erwin Madrid

STONE ARCH BOOKS
a capstone imprint

Dear Diary,

The past few months have been crazy, and not just because I moved across the country. I never thought we'd leave Chicago. The city was home my whole life. I loved the rumbling above-ground trains, the massive skyscrapers, the sidewalks filled with people. . . . Believe it or not, I even liked my school. It was the type of place where it was cool to be smart.

But then, right after school ended for the year, Mom and Dad announced we were moving. They decided to leave their jobs as marine biologists at the Shedd Aquarium and move the whole family to Charleston, South Carolina! They both got jobs running someplace called Seaside Sanctuary Marine Wildlife Refuge—jobs that were "too good to pass up," as they put it.

And at first, I couldn't believe Seaside Sanctuary would ever seem like home. Everything was different— the humidity, the salty air, the palmetto trees, the old brick streets lined with massive live oaks. Not to mention the flat, quiet beaches with water warm enough to swim in all year—you don't see that along Lake Michigan.

But it hasn't all been bad. For starters, I met my best friend, Olivia, on my first day at Seaside Sanctuary. She was sitting by the turtle pool, reading. By the end of the morning, I knew three very important things about Olivia:

1. Her older sister, Abby, is the vet at the sanctuary.
2. She doesn't like talking to people she doesn't know.
3. She wants to be a dolphin researcher when she grows up.

And I knew we were going to be best friends.

I still miss Chicago. But between helping the volunteers with feedings, cleaning tanks, showing tourists around, and prepping seal food in the industrial-sized blender, I haven't had much time to think about my old life. And one thing is for sure—at Seaside Sanctuary, I'm never lonely, and I'm never bored.

Chapter 1

"Elsa, don't forget the emergency release forms,"
Mom said. She bustled around the cluttered office of
Seaside Sanctuary, gathering up stray clipboards.

"Already got them." I waved the stack of forms
I just pulled out of the printer.

Getting ready for a new group of volunteers
always required *lots* of paperwork. Today we had five
starting. My best friend, Olivia, and I had agreed

to help with the orientation. Mom needed the assistance. My dad was at a conference, and Abby, Seaside Sanctuary's vet and Olivia's older sister, was off-site taking a pelican to a specialist.

At least we didn't have to get up too early—my house was just a few yards away from the Seaside Sanctuary office, and Olivia and Abby lived in the apartment right above it.

"It's nine, girls!" Mom called, disappearing out the office door. Olivia grabbed the clipboards, and together we trotted down the path to the main entrance.

The volunteers were already gathered near the turtle habitat, waiting for us. I counted five in total: a middle-aged couple, an older-looking lady, a boy in a black sweatshirt with the hood up, and a lady in bright purple leggings.

"Hi, everyone!" Mom greeted them. "We're so happy to have you here at Seaside Sanctuary. We couldn't survive without our volunteers. You're all very important to our work. Why doesn't everyone introduce themselves and then we'll give you a tour?"

The middle-aged couple went first and introduced themselves as Jeffrey and Rebecca. The older lady was Paula.

"I'm Megan," the purple-leggings lady announced in a loud voice. She flashed a huge smile at the group and a dimple appeared in her cheek. She ran a hand through her long, curly hair. "I'm so excited to be here. I *love* animals! I can't *wait* to see all the adorable babies!"

Mom smiled politely. "We don't actually have any babies right now. But we are certainly glad to have you here, Megan." With that, she turned to the boy in the black hoodie, who hadn't said anything. "And what about you? Can you tell us your name?"

The boy mumbled something. He kept his face down so that only his eyes and forehead were visible.

Mom leaned closer. "I'm sorry, what did you say? It might be easier to hear you if you put your hood down."

The boy angrily shoved his hood off his head. "I *said* my name is Anson!"

I stifled a gasp. Part of the boy's face was badly scarred. A patch of shiny burn tissue covered one cheek and part of his mouth, extending up to his scalp. His greasy brown hair was long and stringy, hanging down over his forehead.

Mom looked taken aback too. "Oh, I'm sorry." She dropped the papers off her clipboard, and I quickly crouched to help her pick them up. Anson pulled his hood back up so it hid his face.

"OK, it's time for our tour!" Mom announced. She seemed to have regained her composure.

"Elsa and Olivia know the sanctuary inside out, and they're much more fun to listen to, so I'll let them lead us."

"Oh, lovely!" Megan piped up from the front. "Do you happen to have any arowana fish? I understand they're very interesting."

Mom frowned slightly. "No, we don't have any arowana fish. We don't keep exotic fish here. Arowana are mainly kept as pets. We only rehabilitate and house marine mammals native to this part of South Carolina."

"OK, let's go!" I said. I led the group around the turtle habitat and past the freshwater birds—three ducks were in there now. Then I took them past the ocean birds, where one lone pelican was standing on a rock beside his pool.

"This guy was found on the beach with a damaged wing," Olivia explained. "But we think he'll heal enough to be released."

We headed to the wild pen with the dolphins next. "This is one of the few wild pens in the country," I told the group. "We had to get a special federal permit to build it. Seaside Sanctuary is a perfect fit for a coastal pen because we have a natural cove; the other side has netting to keep the dolphins in. This is healthier for them than a pool."

I also explained the feeding process—that we used only fresh fish from a restaurant-supply company and that they were all inspected before being fed to the dolphins—before moving on.

"And these are our river otters," I said, stopping at the big habitat we'd built for them. "They just arrived a couple of weeks ago. Their mom was hit by a boat and killed. The boatman brought us her pups."

I motioned to the five little otters swimming in their pool, diving and doing somersaults. One of them pushed a big red ball around in the water.

"Oooh," the group said, swooning over the otters.

I had to agree. The otters were insanely cute. They looked like furry old men with their little eyes and big soft noses and long whiskers. But in the water, they transformed into swimming machines, streaking through the pool like sleek brown torpedoes.

"These are otters, but they're not sea otters," I explained. People often made that mistake. "Sea otters live in the sea—obviously. They're the ones with big eyes who lie on their backs and swim. These are river otters. They live in either freshwater or brackish water, like in the intracoastal waterways here in Charleston. They're really smart and really playful. They eat all kinds of fish, crabs, and crayfish. We give them smelt, trout, and herring here, and they get live crabs twice a week."

As we watched, two of the otters climbed out of the pool onto their rocks. Everyone *ooohed* again.

"They get out of the water quite a bit, as you can see," I went on. "They actually spend a lot of time on land, resting and sleeping and eating. And then they get back in the water."

"Oh, how sweet!" Megan exclaimed. She tottered forward on white platform sneakers and bent over, her bottom sticking out toward us. "Babies! Here! Over here, babies!" She tapped the fence with a long pink fingernail.

"Ah, please don't tap the fence," Mom said. "We try not to treat the animals here like pets. It's important to remember they are wild creatures and should be respected as such."

I wasn't sure how much of this little speech Megan took in, because she continued to croon at the otters, who were ignoring her.

"They're not stupid either," Anson muttered from the back of the group. "Unlike you."

I gasped before I could stop myself. He glared at me from under the edge of his hood. Luckily for him, no one else seemed to have heard except for Olivia, who gave me a *What the heck?* look.

"Why is he being so mean?" Olivia whispered as the volunteers crowded around the habitat. Anson stood back, hands in his pockets. "He's here to volunteer, isn't he? He doesn't seem like he wants to be here at all."

"I know," I whispered back. "It's weird. He doesn't even seem to like the animals."

So why was he? I didn't know, yet, but I was sure going to figure it out.

Chapter 2

"Brownies, everyone!" a voice called the next morning.

Olivia and I looked at each other. She turned off the hose she'd been using to clean algae off the pelican's pool, and I set down my scrubbing brush. We headed toward the otter habitat to find Megan taking a plate of brownies out of a larger plastic tub. It was one of those big twenty-gallon bins, the kind you'd use to store balls or tennis rackets in your garage, and almost comically large.

Maybe she had more than one thing of brownies in there, I thought as I watched Megan arrange the brownies on a rack next to a pile of feeding tubes.

The other volunteers, all clad in their gray Seaside Sanctuary T-shirts, were clustered around Mom. She was explaining how to sort the fish for the river otters. Anson stood at the back, like yesterday. He'd pulled his T-shirt over his black sweatshirt, which gave him a lumpy look. Plus he must have been hot. It was like eighty-five degrees.

"Thanks, Megan," I said, stuffing a brownie in my mouth. "That's really nice of you."

"Oh it's nothing!" She waved her hand in the air. Today her leggings were aqua with big swirls of purple. "Just a little something I whipped up!"

"Elsa!" Mom waved Olivia and me over. "I moved the otters to their holding area." She motioned to the small, fenced-off section we kept the otters in if we needed to be in the habitat.

"I want you two to lead the group in cleaning the habitat, OK? Then Anson is going to help you with some training. Abby is over at the West Side Clinic today, so it's just you guys."

"Mom, not Anson!" I did *not* want to work with that grumpy guy. He was scary.

She bent over. "I think Anson needs a little extra attention to feel welcome here. And you're a great teacher. I'm sure he'll enjoy the training."

"All right, all right," I muttered.

"Maybe he'll have cheered up from yesterday," Olivia whispered hopefully.

"Doesn't look like it," I whispered back, shooting a glance at Anson.

Back at the enclosure, I let the group into the habitat, which was filled with everything otters like: lots of rocks, logs, shrubs, sticks. The otters

had already made a den in a rock crevice. The pool
was lined with rocks and surrounded by clay and
rocks so the otters could scamper in and out of the
water.

I handed out brushes, small shovels, and
buckets. "OK, guys. We're going to be picking
up all the droppings, plus any litter you see, and
putting them in the buckets," I explained. "And
then we have to scrub the algae off the stones.
They're too slippery for the otters otherwise."

Without a word, Anson grabbed a bucket
and a shovel and went off to the far corner of the
exhibit, pulling his hood up to shield his face again.
The others got to work—except for Megan, who
wandered off to the otters' holding area. The five
of them clustered at the fence, watching us with
their bright little eyes.

"Oh, they're so beautiful!" Megan wiggled her
fingers at them. "How old are they?"

"Um, five months." I raked through a section of dirt and tossed a pile of droppings into the bucket Olivia held out for me. "They're weaned now, but we bottle-fed them when they first got here."

"Are they males or females? You're sure they're river otters?"

"Yes, they are, and I can't remember if they're males or females." I edged away, hoping she'd get the hint and get to work. "Well, it's time for scrubbing."

Megan absently picked up a brush from the pile, but her eyes were still fixed on the otters.

"She really loves otters," Olivia said quietly.

"Tell me about it." I nudged her. "Hey, look."

The other volunteers were scrubbing, working slowly as they chatted and looked around, talking about the animals. But Anson was on the other side of the pond, alone. He was scrubbing deliberately, not looking up, cleaning each stone all over before he moved on to the next one.

We watched him in silence for a few minutes. "Well, at least he's not a slacker," I said finally.

"OK!" Mom called from outside the pen. "Thank you, everyone! If you could all gather over here, I'd like to go over a few items from yesterday. Olivia, could you help me, please? Anson, I'd like you to assist Elsa."

I sighed and secured the habitat gate as the other volunteers filed out. Anson slouched up and stood silently beside me. I tried not to look at his scarred face.

"You're a good cleaner," I said, trying to break the ice.

He shrugged. So much for that.

I picked up the bucket of fish Mom had left for me and opened the enclosure gate. The otters tottered out, running all around us.

"We have to handle them every day," I told him. "It helps us check them for any sickness or injuries.

Plus it keeps them used to us, so we can move them around and the vet can see them."

Anson didn't respond. I didn't know why I was bothering to explain any of this. It was like talking to a lump.

I held a fish out to the nearest otter, a female I'd been calling Little Sister. She sniffed it and took a delicate bite, then I drew my hand straight up. That was the signal to stand on her hind feet.

"Why are you doing that?" Anson asked. I jumped. I'd almost forgotten he was there.

"Oh, it helps their muscles get strong. And I can see her belly to check if she has any cuts or anything."

"Cool." Anson drew closer. He gazed at the otter and reached a tentative finger toward her damp, thick fur. "I had a dog once." He spoke so quietly that I had to lean down to catch his words. "Buddy. His fur was almost this exact color."

I held the fish in my hand out to him. I don't know why I did it. But he took the fish and held it out to the otter.

"Break off a little chunk and hold it right up to her mouth," I said quietly.

He followed my directions, and Little Sister took a dainty bite and nibbled. "She ate it!" Anson looked over at me, his face lit up.

I grinned despite myself and nodded. "You did great. You were quiet—they like that. Some people get all giggly and nervous. But you were calm."

Anson seemed to grow about three inches. "Thanks."

"Elsa!" Olivia called to me. "Paula scraped her arm. I can't find the first aid kit. Do you know where it is?"

"Hang on, I think it's in the office." I opened the gate. "Oh you should come out too. I can't leave you alone in the exhibit."

"Could I sit here just for a minute?" Anson asked, gazing at the otters. "I won't touch them, I promise."

"Elsa!" Olivia called again.

"Um . . . OK," I said. It was probably fine. I'd be right back after all.

I hurried off, almost bumping into Megan on my way out the gate.

"Oops!" She giggled. "Just looking for the bathroom."

"Um, it's way over there," I said, pointing. Mom had told all the volunteers where it was earlier, so either Megan hadn't listened or she had a terrible memory.

"Got it, thanks!" Megan chirped, hurrying off.

In the office, Olivia and I got Paula patched up. Just as we were putting the first aid kit back, I saw some kind of commotion happening through the office window. Megan was by the gate now, gesturing wildly toward the parking lot. My dad was trying to talk to her. He must have come down from the office—I hadn't seen him all morning.

We ran outside just as Dad was walking away. He came toward us, looking flustered. "Can you girls keep an eye on everyone down here, please? Megan's car won't start. I need to call roadside assistance."

Just then Anson appeared beside me. "What's going on?"

I did a double take. "I thought you were with the otters," I said quietly, not wanting Dad to overhear that I'd left a volunteer alone.

Anson cleared his throat. "I, uh, overheard you guys talking about a car problem. I could look at it. Maybe. If you want, I mean. I work on my dad's car sometimes."

"Well, thanks," I said slowly. Olivia and I looked at each other, both clearly surprised by the offer. He didn't seem as mean or scary as yesterday.

"Yes, thank you," Dad echoed. He gave Anson a distracted smile. "That would be very helpful."

Out in the parking lot, Megan was pacing around her car, clearly fuming. She started talking the minute she saw us.

"I don't know why it won't start! This car is new!" she practically yelled. "I have to be somewhere—I can't be stuck at this dump for three hours!"

Beside me, Olivia bristled, but I forced myself to stay calm. Seaside Sanctuary wasn't a dump, and we knew it. Anson simply popped the hood and stuck his head under it.

"I'm sure your car will start any minute," I said, trying to soothe her. "Anson knows everything about cars." I hoped that was true, at least.

Just then a movement inside the car caught my eye. I leaned closer. A large yellow cat with black markings was pacing back and forth on the backseat. It was at least three times larger than a housecat, and its beautiful black markings made it look like a mini tiger. It reminded me of some exotic cat from an Egyptian tomb.

"Is that cat yours?" Olivia asked, leaning around me and trying to get a closer look through the tinted window.

"No." Megan moved swiftly in front of us, almost knocking me off my feet. "She belongs to a friend. I'm just taking care of her."

The sudden roar of the engine startled all of us. Anson emerged, wiping his hands on his jeans. "One of your battery cables was loose. I just tightened it up."

"Oh thank you! Thank you so much!" Megan jumped in her car, barely looking at us. As she roared out of the parking lot, I could just see the cat's long tail visible through the car's rear window.

Suddenly a shout came from the otter enclosure. I ran toward it, Anson close behind me. The other volunteers looked up from their work, their eyes wide. My parents were inside the otter enclosure, all looking wild-eyed.

"What? What is it?" I cried.

Dad didn't answer. He was rummaging in the shrubs inside the habitat.

But Mom came over, her face serious. "One of the otters is missing," she said. "We don't know where he is."

Chapter 3

We held a staff meeting after all the volunteers went home. Mom and Dad were grim-faced, and Olivia's eyes were red from crying. I felt sick. I couldn't stop thinking of the young male otter, out there somewhere in the world, lost and afraid.

Abby had returned from the clinic and had gotten the bad news. She went over the facts once again. "We've looked at the fencing and the walls, and we can't find any holes or cracks he could have slipped through. That's not likely anyway. If one of their littermates had slipped out, the others would have followed. It's possible he slipped out while the gate was open. But I think someone would have seen him." Abby turned to me. "Elsa, you were in and out of the enclosure the most. Is it possible the otter got out without you seeing him?"

I thought carefully, then shook my head. "When Anson and I were in there handling them there were definitely five. I remember because we talked about the number. Then I went out to help Paula with her arm, and Anson asked . . ." Suddenly a terrible feeling came over me. "Anson asked if he could stay in the enclosure with the otters," I said slowly.

I looked at everyone's faces. I could see what they were all thinking. Only Olivia was brave enough to voice it.

"Could someone have *taken* the otter?" she asked tremblingly. I noticed she didn't say *Anson*.

"I think we have to at least consider the possibility," Mom said. She shook her head. "What a terrible thought—a thief at Seaside Sanctuary!"

"But *why* would someone take a river otter?" Dad asked, pushing his reading glasses up on his head. "It's not a diamond or a wallet. It's an animal!"

The sun was setting, sending long red rays through the dusty window. "It's dinnertime," Mom said. "We'll keep searching. Maybe we're overreacting, and he'll turn up after all."

But I think all of us knew that wasn't going to happen.

৵৹

The next morning started off badly. For starters, it was raining—a Charleston rain with the water blowing in off the ocean, mixing with salt spray. And, worse, the fish fridge broke down. That was a big deal at Seaside Sanctuary, since the fridge held most of our animal food.

Dad woke me at dawn, hustled me and Olivia down to the kitchen, and told us to get all the food we could into coolers before it spoiled. Then, before I knew it, he and Mom were gone to buy a new fridge, promising to be back before dinner. They thought they might have to go all the way to Columbia, more than two hours away, to find the kind we needed.

We'd been working for a while, the rain slapping the windows, and had the fridge almost emptied when a figure darkened the doorway.

"Anson!" Olivia exclaimed as I looked up.

"Hi." He wore the same black hoodie he'd been wearing for the past two days. But despite the rain, he didn't look that wet. Just a few drops splotched his shoulders and head. He slouched on a stool near the door, watching us.

I didn't know why he was here. The volunteers weren't due for another couple hours. I wondered again if he'd had anything to do with the missing otter. But why would he take *otters?* Why not just take the money we had in the office cash box?

"Why are you guys doing that?" he finally asked.

I pointed at the silent fridge, sitting with its door hanging open. "It's kaput. Dad found it this morning."

"So what?" Anson said. "It's just a fridge."

"It's more than that," I said. "We keep all the mammal food in here, including the fish. My parents went to buy another one, but we need a special kind. And they're really expensive."

Anson stared at us a long moment, his eyes half closed. Then he heaved himself off the stool. "Here," he said abruptly, shoving us aside. "Gimme a screwdriver."

Olivia and I looked at each other, and then she opened a drawer and dug out a screwdriver. Anson wrestled the front plate off the fridge and did something to the underside, lying on his back on the sticky linoleum floor.

Suddenly the fridge coughed, and the room was filled with the smooth hum of a motor.

"You fixed it!" I cried.

Anson grunted and got up.

"You know a lot about fixing things," Olivia said.

He shrugged. "There's a lot of broken stuff at my house. I've had practice."

"Thanks," I said. That was two nice things he'd done in two days.

"How're the otters doing?" he asked. "Did you find the missing one?"

Olivia and I exchanged upset looks. "No, not yet," I said. "But we will." Somehow.

"Well, are you doing more training today? I thought maybe I could help."

"Sure—" I started to say, then stopped myself. Was there more to his offer? Was Anson a thief?

Helping with training *would* be a good way to take an otter. . . .

But why the heck would he take an otter? It seemed like such a weird thing for a teenage boy to steal. Still, he had liked them a lot. Maybe it had something to do with Little Sister reminding him of his dog?

"Forget it," Anson said, seeming to sense my hesitation.

He was halfway out the door before I jerked myself out of my thoughts, "Hey, wait!" I hurried after him, Olivia close behind.

We skidded to a halt at the otter enclosure, the light rain pelting our heads and necks. I was surprised to see Megan outside the fence. Her big plastic storage tub from the other day sat outside the otter gate. I hadn't realized anyone else was here, other than Abby, who was all the way down in the cove, working with the dolphins.

Maybe she brought us more brownies, I thought hopefully.

"How could you?" Megan shrieked as soon as she saw us.

"What?" Olivia asked.

"How could you, you evil boy?" Megan extended a trembling finger at Anson. Her hair was soaking wet and hanging in ropy strings to her shoulders.

"What? Do what?" Anson looked around wildly.

"Megan, calm down," I tried to soothe her.

"He stole an otter!" she screeched.

My heart pounded as I stared into the habitat. Three otter faces stared back at me. Three!

"Olivia, help me!" I scrabbled to unfasten the gate. I ran into the enclosure, tearing at shrubs, peering under logs and rocks.

"She's right!" Olivia gasped. "Another one is gone!"

"How could you?" I hollered at Anson, who was standing frozen outside the gate. He'd pushed his hood back, and his long bangs were plastered to his forehead. "Why are you doing this?" I advanced on him. "Why are you taking them? Where are they?" I was almost yelling in his face.

Anson's expression changed from shocked to angry. "You think I did this?" he snarled. "Well, you would, wouldn't you. You would think that." He stalked away. In seconds, the misty gray rain swallowed him up.

I sagged back against the gate. Another otter was gone. What were we going to do? Had I just let the thief walk away?

"I'll get my sister," Olivia said, hurrying down the path.

"I knew he was a bad one when I saw him," Megan was saying. She swiped at her wet hair and picked up her bin, staggering slightly. "I brought more treats, but we're clearly not in the mood, are we? I'll put this in my car." She lugged it away.

"What happened?" Abby hollered as she came running up, Olivia close behind. "Another otter is gone?"

"Oh, Abby!" I wailed. "Those poor otters! Do you think it's a thief like Mom said? Do you think it's Anson?"

"I don't know." Abby wrapped an arm around me, and we walked toward the office.

"He's so weird—nice one minute, fixing things, and then yelling the next minute," Olivia put in.

"What're Mom and Dad going to say? We lost another otter!" Warm tears spilled down my cheeks, mixing with the cold rain. "What are we going to do?"

"I don't know, but this isn't helping," Abby muttered as she spotted Megan coming toward us.

She flapped down the path, breathing hard, her cheeks red.

Abby steered us into the office, and I sank down on the office chair as Olivia tossed a torn towel into my lap. Megan followed us, undeterred.

"I knew that boy was up to no good," Megan said breathlessly. "I knew it the moment I saw him. I have a nose for it, you know. I always have. Thank goodness I came in early to bring treats. Who knows how many he might have taken if I hadn't spotted him and—"

"Megan—" Abby cut off her monologue. "What did you see, exactly? Did you *see* Anson taking an otter?"

"Er, well . . ." Megan shuffled some papers on Dad's desk. "Not *exactly*. I don't know what I saw. There was someone in the enclosure, but the rain was so heavy. And then an otter was gone!" She looked up, her face covered with ruined makeup.

"Who else was here, hmm? It had to be him."
She stood up, her confidence returning.

"But you *did* see someone in the enclosure?"
I asked.

"Yes." She nodded vigorously. "I'm certain that
I did."

Olivia's eyes met mine. There was an otter thief
at Seaside Sanctuary. And I wasn't looking forward
to telling Mom and Dad who it was.

Chapter 4

We heard Mom and Dad's truck pull in an hour later. I'd texted them to let them know that Anson had fixed the fridge—but that we had a bigger problem now. They'd rushed straight back to Seaside Sanctuary. The rain had stopped by the time they arrived, and the setting sun was sending watery rays over the ocean. Everything was gray and wet, which just about matched my mood.

"Elsa!" Mom's voice came from down the path.

"Mom, I'm here," I called from inside the otter habitat. I'd gone in to spend some time with the remaining otters. Olivia had already gone to her and Abby's apartment over the office. I needed to talk to Mom on my own.

Mom pushed the gate open and came inside. "Another otter! I can't believe it!"

"Mom, I'm so sorry," I said quietly. "I don't know what happened."

Mom passed her hand over her forehead and rubbed as though she had a headache. Then she sat down on a rock and motioned me over to sit beside her. Together we watched the three remaining otters playing—running in and out of the water, pushing their big red ball around with their muzzles, chasing each other.

Otters love to be with each other. They're always playing. My heart ached thinking of the two that were missing. Were they alone and scared? Did whoever took them even know what to feed them? What if they gave them the wrong food? Did they have enough water?

"OK," Mom finally said. "Tell me what you know."

Quickly I brought Mom up to speed on what had happened while she was gone. There'd been too much to text.

"Megan was here, and she's accusing Anson of stealing the otters," I said. "She says she didn't see him, exactly, but she did see someone in the habitat. And there wasn't anyone else here."

Mom listened intently. When I was done, she sighed and looked across at the otters. The sun was starting to set, which meant they'd be denning up soon. People sometimes think otters make little nests, but that's not true. They just crowd in under whatever spot they like—

overhanging rock, hollow log, that sort of thing. They don't really scratch out beds like some small mammals.

Mom sighed. "I hate to say it, but I think Anson is involved. He's been here both times the otters have disappeared. The first time, he was right in the enclosure."

"But the second time, he was here in the office," I said. I felt strangely upset.

"You don't know what he was doing before he showed up in the office, do you?" Mom said quietly. "You told me yourself that the rain was making it hard to hear outside. He could have gone to the enclosure and taken the otter first."

"But he fixed the fridge," I protested. "And Megan's car."

"That was nice of him, but it doesn't have anything to do with the otters disappearing. And honestly, Elsa, his attitude has been pretty unpleasant. We have to ask ourselves why he's here in the first place. He certainly doesn't seem to *want* to be here."

I jumped up from the rock. "He does! He likes the otters, I can tell! He just doesn't . . . express himself very well. He's really a good guy, Mom." I didn't even realize I had come to this conclusion until I heard myself saying it.

Mom shook her head. "You're a kind person, Elsa, but this is something your father and I need to handle ourselves." She stood up, signaling that the conversation was over.

"What are you going to do now?" I asked desperately.

"We'll need to notify the police, but I need to talk to Abby first. And the board, I suppose. That will take a few days. In the meantime, we need to keep a close eye on the otters and all the animals. There *cannot* be any more thefts at Seaside Sanctuary."

It got worse the next morning at breakfast. I came downstairs to find Mom's iPad on the breakfast table, right between the jam and the plate of toast. Mom was boiling the kettle at the stove, and Dad was reading *Proceedings of the Society of Marine Biology* with his glasses pushed up on his head.

I sat down and pulled the iPad toward me. It was open on an article: "Local Boy Arrested for Theft" the headline read. It was dated a couple months ago.

Quickly, I scanned it, reading aloud. "A local boy, age thirteen, was arrested Thursday afternoon for stealing change out of unlocked cars on East Bay Street in downtown Charleston. He was discovered by police and released to his parents."

I looked at Mom and Dad. "What is this?" I asked.

My parents exchanged a look. "I'm afraid it's Anson," Mom said gently. "Apparently he has a history of stealing."

"What?" I exclaimed. "How do you know that? You can't be sure this is about him. It could be anyone!"

"Abby has a friend who works at the sheriff's office," Mom replied. "She asked around for us after I told her about what happened yesterday. It's him."

"I wish we'd never laid eyes on the kid," Dad said, sounding furious. "If he's taken two otters . . . I don't want him back here, you understand, Elsa? He's not to set foot in Seaside Sanctuary."

"Dad, you can't just kick him out!" I shoved the iPad away from me. "I don't think he's the thief. I just don't. He's really nice once you get to know him. You guys just haven't spent as much time with him as I have."

"Elsa, 'nice' has nothing to do with this situation," Dad said. "Valuable animals are missing, and this boy has a history of stealing!"

"So he made a mistake once! Haven't you ever made a mistake? It's a big jump from stealing change to stealing otters. And *why* would he steal otters, anyway? Why wouldn't he just sneak into the office and take the cash box?" Now I was getting mad. I shoved my chair back, making it screech against the linoleum. "I think it's awful of you to keep him off the grounds. It's-it's . . ." I searched for the right word. "Discrimination!"

"Calm down," Mom said sharply. "Yelling like this will get us nowhere." She turned to Dad. "Warren, let's not be too hasty. Let him on the grounds, but we'll keep him under close supervision. Perhaps some more information will come to light this week. It would be good to have a solid case for the authorities." She fixed me with a stare. "But Elsa, you need to know this: we *will* be talking to the police at the end of the week."

I scrambled out of the room, stifling a sob, and went in search of Olivia. I found her in her apartment, hunched over her laptop. I snuck a look at the screen. She'd been Googling *river otters.*

"Finding anything?" I sat down beside her.

She sighed. "Just trying to see if the otters will be OK if whoever has them isn't taking very good care of them."

I leaned over her shoulder. "Will they? Does it say why anyone will steal an otter?"

Olivia shook her head. "I can't find out why anyone would steal an otter, but it does say that even though otters spend tons of time in water, they'd still be OK for a long time on land. They might not be very happy or healthy, but they won't die if whoever has them doesn't give them a place to swim."

"That's good, I guess." I paused, then forced myself to say something that had been on my mind for a while. "If they're still alive."

"What?"

I made myself say the words. "The otters. We've been acting like of course they're alive somewhere, but what if whoever took them . . ."

"Killed them," Olivia finished, looking horrified.

She turned back to the computer, scrolling down the list of search results. Then she pointed at the computer screen, to an article on fur-bearing animals: minks, martens, rabbits, and otters. Animals that are trapped and killed for their fur.

We stared at each other. The thought was too terrible to linger on. That couldn't be it. The otters were out there, and they were alive. I had to believe that.

"Olivia, I don't think Anson is the thief." Quickly I filled her in on Anson's past. "I know it looks bad, but I just don't think he would do it. He loves those otters."

She nodded. "I agree with you on that. I don't think he'd put them in danger. But . . ."

I knew what she was thinking. "But if Anson *isn't* the otter thief, then we have to find out who is."

Olivia nodded again and thought for a minute. "We have to talk to him," she said finally. "I don't know if he's involved or not, but we should at least tell him what's going to happen at the end of the week. And who knows? Maybe he'll have some ideas."

Chapter 5

Thirty minutes of hard walking brought us to a little wooden house at the end of Burnt Cabin Road. Walls of bright pink and purple azalea flowers crowded the driveway. The live oak trees arched overhead, blocking most of the sunshine. A little girl sat on a tricycle in the front yard.

This place didn't look like anywhere I'd seen in Charleston so far. But I remembered Mom had told me that some of the houses back in the country had been there since way before the Civil War. This definitely looked like one of them.

"Is Anson here?" I asked the little girl. She got off her trike and ran into the house. A moment later, a figure appeared at the screen door.

"Hi!" I called. "It's Elsa and Olivia!"

Anson pushed the screen door open and came out onto the porch. He wore a torn white T-shirt instead of his black hoodie. It was the first time I'd seen him without it, I realized. He looked skinnier than I'd thought and strangely exposed, like a crab without a shell.

"What?" His voice was as flat and hostile as ever, but I knew enough now not to let that bother me.

"Anson, we've got trouble. It's about the otters."

"I didn't take them!" His voice rose and suddenly he looked back over his shoulder and motioned us around the side of the house, which stood on short stilts. It was propped up that way, I knew, in case the waterways flooded.

"Listen, I believe you," I said right away, before he could start shouting again.

He blinked. "You do?"

"Yeah," Olivia said. "I was thinking about it last night. We can tell you really like animals, and we don't think someone who loved the otters that much would steal them. It would put them in danger, and you wouldn't want that. Besides, what would you do with them? Keep them under your bed?"

Anson visibly relaxed. "That's what I wanted to say yesterday. I'm sorry I stormed off. I should've stayed."

"The problem is that my parents found out about you stealing change out of people's cars." I filled him in on the rest of my parents' decisions, including telling the police.

"No!" Anson's eyes widened. "Please don't let them go to the police! Look, I did steal stuff out of people's cars. I don't even know why I did it. It was stupid. I'm sorry I did it, and I've never done anything like that before or since. But my parents said that if I get in any more trouble, they'll send me away to my Uncle Bruce's place upstate. Please! You guys have to help me!"

"OK, OK, calm down," I said. I led him over to the splintery back steps, and we all sat down. "We're not going to let you go upstate. But we need to find a way to prove you're not the thief. Because you have to admit, it looks a little suspicious. I mean, you show up, you're with the otters both times they disappear, you're kind of . . ." I paused, not wanting to offend him. "Well, you're not the friendliest volunteer we've ever had."

Anson's face went red. "So what? It's a crime to not be friendly?" he mumbled. "I have a hard time around new people. But I didn't have anything to do with the otters disappearing, OK?"

I nodded. "OK. But we need a plan. And since we suspect there *is* an otter thief, the best way to clear your name is to find out who he or she is."

"I think we need to look at the *why*," Olivia piped up. "I mean, an otter isn't like a wallet or a computer or a piece of jewelry. An otter is an animal. It needs food and water. It's going to be a hassle to have around. So I think we need to figure out *why* someone would steal an otter in the first place. And maybe that will help lead us to the thief."

Anson nodded. "OK, let's start at the library. That's always the best place."

I was surprised to hear him say that—he didn't look like the type of boy who spent a lot of time at the library. But then again, I was starting to learn not to let myself be fooled by appearances.

∾

An hour later, the three of us were crouched over a computer at the Charleston Public Library. Anson seemed totally at home in the quiet space.

"Let's Google *river otters* first, to see what's out there," he suggested. His fingers flew over the keys with surprising speed.

"I already did that the other day," Olivia said.

"Might be worth another look," he said.

We all scanned the list that popped up. Sites on the otters' habitats, feeding habits, babies, family groups. Lots of pictures of the little guys. I teared up a little at the sight of their funny old-man faces. I hoped the stolen pair were out there somewhere, and safe.

"Anson, dear, let me know if I can help."

I turned around at the sound of the librarian's voice. She stood behind us, smiling, then patted Anson on the shoulder before walking away.

"You know the librarian?" I asked.

Anson shrugged. "I come in here a lot to read, look things up . . ." He cleared his throat. "We don't have a lot of books at home. Or a computer, for that matter."

Something about the way he said it told me not to ask any more.

Anson cleared his throat. "Here, look at this."

Olivia and I turned our attention back to the screen. "Otters Crowd Tokyo's Wildlife Cafés," I read aloud.

Quickly we scanned the article. It described cafés in Japan, full of animals to pet and play with, where people could go and have fancy drinks. The animals were like entertainment. But they weren't just regular pet-type animals like dogs or cats. The cafés in the article had owls, small exotic cats like ocelots, and *otters*.

"So this place gets animals and basically uses them as entertainment?" Olivia asked.

"Yeah, that seems like the idea," Anson said. "And look, here's another article about these wildlife cafés in general. They're all across Asia and Russia, apparently—and they're really popular."

Suddenly he stopped and leaned closer to the screen. He read for what seemed like a hundred years, his face growing more and more serious.

"What? What?" I gripped the edge of the table and tried to see what he was reading. Beside me, Olivia was gnawing on her fingernails, her eyes fixed on Anson.

Anson finally looked at us, his eyes big. "This article was from a wild-animal watchdog group. It talks about the black-market trade of exotic animals."

"Black market? That means illegal, right?" I asked.

He nodded. "Right, like animals bought and sold against the law. Anyway, it says that the wildlife cafés in Asia and Russia are a big part of it. Most of the animals there were bought on the black market."

I took the mouse from Anson and scrolled through some of the pictures. Well-dressed people sat around a candy-colored café. There were caged animals on each side and other animals, including otters, walking around on the floor. People were taking selfies with the otters and drinking foamy-looking drinks.

It didn't look anything like Seaside Sanctuary. It didn't look like any kind of place for animals. There were no pools to swim in, no bushes to hide in, no logs to den under. I wanted to cry, thinking of our otters in a place like that.

Olivia read my mind. "OK, so that's *one* place our otters could have gone. We've been asking why someone would go to the trouble of stealing two otters. But I guess they're part of this exotic animal trade. But how do we know for sure? I mean, they could be anywhere. They could be dead."

Anson's face twisted, and he glared at Olivia. "They're not dead. I don't know where they are, but I know they're not dead," he said.

He couldn't know that, of course, any more than we could, but he looked so fierce that neither of us argued with him.

"We're going to catch this thief," I told him, catching Olivia's eye. She nodded vigorously. "And we're going to clear your name too. You're going to be safe—and so will our otters."

I only wished I felt as sure as I sounded.

Chapter 6

Anson was waiting at the sanctuary's kitchen door the next morning when I came outside. I almost fell over in shock when I saw his grumpy face.

"What are you doing here?" I hissed. "I mean, I know you're innocent and all, but Mom and Dad don't—yet."

Anson shoved his hands deep into his pockets. I could see his fists balled up through the fabric.

"I'm not going to stay away just because I'm falsely accused," he snapped.

"OK, OK, calm down." I held the kitchen door open wider. "Get in here. You can help me inside, and hopefully Mom and Dad won't see you."

With the door closed behind us, I went back to piling herring into our industrial blender. "Here, you can examine the fish, then hand them to me. There can't be any missing eyes or holes in their bodies."

"Why?" Anson asked. "What are you doing?"

"They can't have missing eyes or anything because the holes could have let bacteria in. That would obviously be bad for the animals," I explained. "And I'm making fish milkshakes for the animals who are too sick to eat solid food. We have to tube-feed them."

I plopped a few herring I'd already inspected in the blender and poured in distilled water and a vitamin mixture. I pressed *blend* and watched as the concoction whirled into gray mush.

Anson wrinkled his nose. "And do they like that? The tube, I mean? I wouldn't like someone jamming a tube down my throat and force-feeding me."

"No," I admitted. "I don't think they like it very much. But it's the only way they can eat. They'll die otherwise."

"Well, if it's that or death . . . ," Anson said. He took a herring out of the cooler and started examining it. "Hey, um . . . I don't think I told you and Olivia yet . . . uh, thank you."

I glanced at him. His ears were pink. "Thank you for what?" I asked, dumping the gray mush into a plastic pitcher.

"For, you know, believing I'm innocent. When no one else does." He looked down, seeming embarrassed. The words seemed almost stuck in his throat.

I held my hand out for more herring. "I do believe you. Everyone else is just stupid for thinking you'd be involved with stealing the otters." I paused. "But to be honest, you don't exactly make it easy." I'd been trying to think of a way to tell him this for a while now.

"What do you mean?" he asked, scowling at me.

"Well like that, for instance." I gestured at his face. "You're a really nice guy, but you're always frowning and being sort of grumpy to people. It makes it hard to see the nice part of you."

Anson's scowl deepened. "That's just how my face looks."

"It is not! I've seen you smile. Just not around people like my mom and dad. Herring, please." I accepted three more and dumped them in the blender. "And another thing!" I shouted over the whirr of the motor. "That sweatshirt."

Anson looked down at himself. "What's wrong with this sweatshirt? It's my favorite."

I shut off the blender. "It's not the sweatshirt, exactly. It's just that you wear it all the time, and you always pull the hood up. It's like you're trying to hide from something. And it makes you look sort of scary."

"Well . . . I . . . um," Anson floundered. "It's just that sometimes I think people won't like me. Especially if they see my scars. It's easier to keep them hidden. I don't know. . . . The sweatshirt feels sort of like a shell. You know, like a turtle."

"Um, how did you get them? The scars, I mean? If you don't mind me asking." I stumbled a little over the words. I'd been wanting to ask him, but I didn't want to seem rude.

"I was camping with my family, and my brother tripped me. I fell into the campfire." He shrugged. "It was a long time ago, but people aren't always the nicest about them. Kids used to call me 'alien,' that sort of thing."

I understood better now. "OK, I'm your friend, right? You trust me? Remember how I've been sticking up for you?"

He nodded warily.

"Well, can we do an experiment?" I asked.

"What, like mixing things together?" He edged away from me as if I might leap at him.

"No, not like that. An experiment to make the outside of you match the inside. First, take off your sweatshirt," I instructed.

He clutched at it.

"Come on! It's like eighty degrees outside,"
I said.

"Fine." He unzipped the sweatshirt and peeled it off. Underneath he wore a surprisingly clean and new-looking *Charleston County Library Reads Week!* T-shirt.

He looked down at it when he saw my double take. "Mrs. Gaud gave it to me when we were leaving the other day," he muttered.

"The librarian?" I asked.

He nodded. "She's a friend of mine."

"Cool. But we have to continue with our makeover. Now, stand up straight, instead of all hunched over," I said.

He straightened his back.

"Great, stay that way. Now, smile," I said.

He bared his teeth.

"Not like that. You look like a dinosaur. A real smile," I instructed. "Think of when we were doing the training with Little Sister."

A big grin brightened his face. I'd never noticed before, but his eyes crinkled up when he smiled.

"So much better," I said. But something was still off. "Wait. Hold on." I opened one of the drawers and dug out an old hairbrush. "Here, use this."

"For what?" he asked.

I rolled my eyes. "Your hair."

With a sigh, Anson took the brush and combed his long, stringy hair off his face and back into a neat, short ponytail at the back of his head. I handed him a hair tie I found in my pocket, and he secured his hair.

"OK, now stand up and face me and smile again."

He did as I said. I surveyed him. It was amazing. He looked like a completely different person. He stood up tall, in a clean T-shirt, with a nice smile I could actually see.

"Wow. OK, now the second part. Pretend I'm my mom, and it's your first day at Seaside Sanctuary." I straightened my own shoulders and cleared my throat. "Hello! Are you here to volunteer?" I asked in my most Mom-like voice.

Anson scowled at me and said nothing.

I threw my arms wide. "See? That's what I mean! You just look angry and grumpy. And unfriendly."

"What am I supposed to say?" he asked, with a hint of desperation in his voice.

"Try this: 'Hi! Yes, I am. Thanks for having me. I'm excited to get started.'" I motioned to him. "Go ahead."

Anson rolled his eyes. "No one talks like that. They'd get beat up," he mumbled. But then he took a deep breath and said, "Hi!"

"Stand up straight and smile while you talk," I interrupted him.

He gave me a dirty look. "Hi!" he started again. "I'm here to volunteer. Thanks for having me. I'm excited to get started." He gave me a toothy grin.

"Other than looking like an alligator about to eat a sandpiper, that was really great!" I said. "I'm telling you, if you just smile and talk like a nice, normal person—and stop looking like you hate the world—then everyone else, including my parents, will see what *I* see. The real you."

Anson sank back down on the stool. "I get it. You're right. It's just . . . it's hard to meet people sometimes. To be in new situations. It seems like they're always staring at me—at my scars." He shifted in his seat. "I-I didn't tell you why I came to Seaside Sanctuary in the first place. My parents made me come out here, to volunteer. It was like community service after I got busted stealing change out of those cars. They thought it would be good for me, but I didn't want to come, at all. That's why I was acting so obnoxious at first. But the truth is, I really like animals. I just haven't been around very many before."

"Well, I'm really glad you did." I sat down beside him. "And don't worry. Before we're done, everyone else is going to be glad too. We just have to convince them."

Chapter 7

"Elsa!" Olivia called. "I have to talk to you!"

I opened the door and herded her inside, then shut it quickly. "Hey, have you seen my parents?"

"They're at a donor meeting, why?" she said. Then she saw Anson. "Ohhh. Got it. Don't worry, they went to some restaurant in town for it. They won't be back for a while. Anyway, Anson, I'm glad you're here because this concerns you." She unfolded a thick sheaf of white paper. "I was doing a little research yesterday after we left the library, looking up more about the black-market exotic animal trade and wildlife cafés. And it just seemed like I was getting nowhere." She looked up at us.

"But?" I encouraged her. "I get the feeling you're about to tell us something important."

She held up a finger. "And *then*, I saw this!" She held up her phone in front of us.

I took it from her, and Anson leaned in to see. She had the same article from yesterday pulled up, the one with the photos of the Tokyo café. Same people drinking foamy drinks, same exotic animals walking around on the floor.

"And?" I said.

Olivia tapped her finger on one of the pictures. "Look at that cage in the corner."

I zoomed in closer. A lean, elegant cat was walking around in a cage—it was partly blurred, as if the animal had been in motion when the photo was taken. It looked larger than a house-cat and colored almost like a mini-leopard.

"It's beautiful, but so what?"

"That cat is called an ocelot," she continued. "They live mostly in South America now, and they're very rare in the United States. They used to be hunted for their fur. Between that and the loss of their habitat, you just don't find them in the wild in the U.S. They're considered exotic animals—most states ban owning them as pets. Which is why they're also *really* valuable on the black market."

Olivia paused, and I began to get an inkling of where she was going. "I knew I'd seen a cat like her before," Olivia went on. "I just couldn't remember where. It was bugging me. Then I remembered—"

My mind had been spinning as Olivia spoke, and I gasped. At the same time we said, "In Megan's car!"

The three of us stared at each other. "So you're saying that Megan bought that ocelot on the black market?" Anson said.

"Or she stole it from somewhere, and is planning to sell it to a place like *this*!" Olivia jabbed her phone so hard I was surprised she didn't crack the screen.

My mind felt as if it was racing ahead of me. I almost couldn't keep up. "And if she has connections to the black market . . ."

"Then who's to say she's not trying to use those connections with *our* otters?" Olivia finished my thought.

"Whoa, whoa." Anson held up his hand. "That's a lot of *ifs*. Just because this lady was driving around with a weird cat in her car doesn't mean she's stealing animals to sell on the black market."

"That's exactly what it could mean!" I almost shouted. I held up a finger. "Number one, this lady we've never seen before shows up here to volunteer."

"We've never seen a lot of our volunteers before," Olivia pointed out.

I frowned at her. "Shh. Listen. Number two, she spends time with otters."

"Again, so do a lot of other people," Olivia chimed in.

"Are you helping me here or not?" I said.

"Sorry, sorry! Just playing devil's advocate." She held up her hands in defense.

"Number three, otters disappear. We find out they're popular on the black market. Number four, that same lady we've never seen before is seen with a black-market animal in her car." I sat back in my chair. "Boom! Megan is an otter thief." I let my arms dangle. "My work here is done."

There was a little silence. "You're forgetting one thing," Olivia said.

"What?"

"Megan is accusing Anson of being the otter thief. Oh, and your parents believe her." She looked at me expectantly.

"That's even more reason we have to prove Megan's the thief! We have to clear Anson's name."

"I just have one question," Anson piped up.

"What's that?" I asked.

"*How* are we going to prove Megan's the thief?" he asked.

"We're going to have to check her house," I replied with more confidence than I felt. "If she's keeping the otters there, that'll be all the proof we'll need."

Just as the words were out of my mouth, the office door banged open. My mom barged in.

"Mom!" I gasped. "I thought you weren't supposed to be home until later."

Her face was grim as she looked back and forth from Olivia to Anson to me. "I was interrupted and had to leave early. I suppose it's a good thing Anson is here. It saves us a trip. The three of you, come with me."

Without another word, she turned on her heel and left the office. The three of us shared an uneasy glance before following. Whatever this was about, it didn't look good.

Chapter 8

We understood when we saw the little knot of people waiting outside the office door: Dad, Megan—and a police officer.

As soon as Anson saw them, he turned to run the other way. I grabbed the back of his T-shirt.

"Nothing is going to make you look guiltier than running away," I hissed. "Remember our practice. Stand up straight. Smile."

"There he is!" Megan shrieked as soon as she saw us.

Dad looked both annoyed and concerned. "Megan, we were called out of our donor meeting by your urgent text. Then we arrive here to find you've called the police to Seaside Sanctuary. This is very serious."

"Yes, it is, ma'am," the officer agreed.

I could feel Anson trembling at my side. He was trying to hide slightly behind me.

"Yes, officer!" Megan narrowed her eyes. "It's come to my notice that *this boy* is a known thief. And he was here when two valuable river otters were stolen. I believe *he* is your thief!" Her voice rose to a hysterical pitch, and she pointed a long pink nail at Anson.

The police officer blinked and took a step back. "I wasn't aware you'd had a robbery here," she said, turning to Mom.

"I . . . we . . ." Mom seemed uncertain. "We've had two otters disappear, but we're not accusing anyone. Right now." She glanced briefly at Anson, who was staring at the ground.

I felt as if I might throw up. Anger rolled in my stomach. How *dare* Megan call the police? Was she trying to throw us off the scent? Well, it wouldn't work.

"Are you the owner of these otters?" the officer asked.

"Yes, we are," Dad said. "They disappeared from their habitat about four days ago. We're still not sure if they were lost or, ah, stolen. But we didn't want to contact the police until we had time to gather more information."

"But the thief is standing right in front of you!" Megan shouted. I could smell her from where I was standing—like armpits and warm perfume.

The police officer frowned at Megan. "I don't know if you're aware, ma'am, but making a false accusation to an officer is a crime in South Carolina. I'd think carefully before you speak."

"Yes, thank you, officer," Mom said. "We're still examining the otter situation. We will certainly let you know if we suspect anyone in particular." She again glanced quickly at Anson. I saw her. I could tell she couldn't help it.

Megan's eyes narrowed. "Well if you want to ignore what's right in front of your face, that's your own problem." Her voice hardened. "I was only trying to help!" She turned and stalked away toward the parking lot.

We all stood there awkwardly. I didn't know where to look, and I could tell no one else did either. Mom and Dad didn't know I'd told Anson they suspected him. And they didn't know we thought Megan was the thief.

We all stood there, hiding things from each other, until Mom muttered something about feeding the pelicans and hurried off. Dad trailed after her as the police officer climbed into her cruiser and took off down the driveway.

I exhaled a giant sigh of relief when they all left.

"What the heck was that?" Olivia asked once we were alone. "Why would Megan get the police involved if she's the thief? Wouldn't she want them to stay away?"

"I wonder if she's doing the opposite," I said. "Trying to throw us off her scent. If she makes a big fuss about Anson, no one will realize the real thief is standing right in front of them."

"The accusation is out there," Olivia said. "The police know. We have to find the otters, and fast, or Anson's going to find himself upstate."

Chapter 9

After a brief powwow, we decided Megan's house was our best bet. We didn't have a lot of other places to look. It wasn't likely she'd be carrying the otters around in her car.

The next morning, before anyone else was awake, Olivia and I snuck into the office and looked up Megan's address in her volunteer file. Then, after breakfast, we casually biked away from the sanctuary. Mom, Dad, and Abby thought we were heading into nearby Mt. Pleasant.

Anson met us at the head of Megan's street, about two miles from the sanctuary. Behind him, the white spires of Charleston's Ravenel Bridge were visible above the flat water of the Cooper River.

"There it is," Anson called softly. "On the left."

We stopped our bikes and stared at the house. It couldn't have looked more ordinary—gray clapboard, white trim, neatly cut front lawn, pineapple-shaped mailbox.

"It doesn't really look like the house of an otter thief," Olivia said.

"Whatever that would look like," I replied. "Maybe the black-market exotic animal trade doesn't pay that well. Come on."

We ditched our bikes behind a clump of bushes and skirted the edge of the yard. There were no cars in the driveway, and I prayed there were none in the garage either.

"Get down!" Anson hissed at us, and we ran low along the side of the house in approved sleuth fashion.

"Ouch!" Olivia tripped over the coils of a garden hose.

"Get up!" I hissed at her. "Are you a sleuth or not?"

"Shh!" Anson motioned us ahead. He'd climbed up on a large wooden chest beside the hose. "Guys, check this out!"

He hopped down, and I climbed up and peeked over the edge of the windowsill. I almost fell off the chest. Inside was a room, which was about the size of a large bathroom, with cages and crates of various sizes lined up across the floor. Feeding bowls and water dishes were scattered around.

I climbed down from the crate, and Olivia climbed up next. "Maybe she really likes . . . pets," she said after a moment.

I gave her a *get real* look. "The question is, where are the otters?"

Just then a thump came within the house. We all gasped and huddled together against the outside wall. After a moment, I gathered the courage to climb back on the chest and peek ever so carefully over the windowsill.

"Oh my gosh!" I almost fell off the chest. Megan was coming in the room, carrying the same big plastic tub she always had brownies in at the sanctuary. It was clearly heavy, since she was struggling a little.

She set it down in the middle of the floor. "There!" I could hear her say faintly.

My breath was coming in little gasps. I pressed my chin to the windowsill. Megan opened the lid of the container. A brown muzzle poked out, first one, and then the other.

"It's them!" I whisper-screamed to the others. "They're alive!"

They crowded up against me. "Are they OK?" Olivia asked at the same time Anson said, "Is Megan there?"

"Yes to both," I whispered. "Shh!"

"Now stay there," Megan said. "We're almost ready." She bustled around the room, gathering up bags of food and papers, then dragged the tub with the otters back out of the room.

"She's taking them somewhere," I hissed down to the others. I hopped silently down from the chest. "Hurry, what are we going to do?"

Just then we heard the unmistakable rumble of a garage door, followed by the purr of a car engine. We all looked at each other, eyes wide.

"She's leaving!" Olivia gasped. "With the otters!"

"Hurry up!" Anson raced to the front of the house with us following him. "We have to follow her!"

Megan was just pulling onto the street as we rounded the corner of the house. We grabbed our bikes from the bushes and pedaled after her as fast as we could. We lost her almost immediately but caught up to her at the first stoplight.

"Come on!" Anson shouted over his shoulder, rocketing into the intersection and narrowly avoiding a garbage truck.

"Be careful!" I shouted at his back. I just hoped Megan didn't check her rearview mirror. With any luck she'd be so focused on getting the otters to wherever they were going that she wouldn't look behind her.

We pedaled furiously down the side of the road, barely keeping Megan's car in sight. Finally her turn signal blinked. We followed her onto a smaller asphalt road, then another, this one lined with empty lots and crumbling gas stations. In a weedy parking lot by a diner, she finally stopped.

Anson braked so fast that I had to swerve to avoid crashing into him. Moving fast, we wheeled our bikes behind an old shipping container sitting in a corner of the parking lot.

"What's she doing here?" Olivia whispered.

"I'm guessing it has something to do with *that*," Anson replied. He pointed at a large white van, the kind a repairman might drive, that had just pulled into the parking lot.

The van came to a stop next to Megan's car. A man in a collared shirt and sunglasses got out. Megan emerged from her car as well.

"Oh my gosh, what's going on?" Olivia dug her fingernails into my shoulder.

The two adults held a low conversation, which we couldn't hear, and then the man stepped around to the back of the van. He swung open the doors. The inside was lined with cages.

"No!" Anson said, too loud for comfort. He started forward.

"Wait!" I grabbed him. "The otters are in Megan's car. If you run over there she could just leap in and drive off. Wait until she takes them out."

"And then?" Olivia asked.

"Then . . . ," I trailed off. Then we'd do something brilliant—I just hadn't thought of it yet.

Chapter 10

From our hiding spot, we watched as Megan opened the back door of her car. With obvious difficulty, she dragged the plastic storage bin out. I winced as it thumped onto the pavement.

The man opened the plastic lid, which I was relieved to see had a few holes punched in it, and looked inside. Then he nodded and replaced the lid.

We had to act. In thirty seconds, those otters would be in the back of that van and bound for a ship across the Atlantic. Or something equally as awful.

"Anson, go back to the road and call the police," I whispered. I held out my cell phone, which I was only supposed to use in case of emergency. This definitely qualified. "Stay there so they can find us. Olivia and I will stall."

"How are you going to do that?" Anson whispered back, already backing toward his bike.

"I don't know, but get going," I said. "We'll think of something."

Anson cast a desperate glance over his shoulder and pedaled off. I held my breath until he was out of sight. Megan and the man hadn't spotted him. They were still focused on the otters. They seemed to be arguing about something—money from what I could hear.

"I told you three thousand!" the man yelled at Megan.

"And I'm telling *you* it's four now. These animals have been causing me a lot of trouble," she snarled back.

The man lifted the bin with the otters and shoved it into the back of his truck. "Too bad," he sneered, throwing an envelope on the pavement at her feet.

"Now! Now!" Olivia said. "He's about to drive away!"

I leapt out from behind the container. "W-wait!" I shouted. I had no idea what I was going to say, but we couldn't wait any longer. "You can't take those otters!"

If I hadn't been so terrified, the surprised looks on Megan and the man's faces would have almost been funny. But my heart was pounding in my ears so loudly I could hardly hear my own words.

"Who is *that*?" the man asked Megan.

"They're from the same sanctuary as the otters," Megan said, staring at us. She looked shocked but also furious. "How did you get here?"

"On bikes," I said, trying to hide the tremble in my voice. "And you're not taking those otters."

Out of the corner of my eye, I saw Olivia come up to stand beside me. "They're not yours," she added. "They belong in our sanctuary."

The man laughed. "OK, whatever." He banged the doors closed on the van.

"Wait!" I cried. I had to do something to stall until Anson returned with the police. "The otters are—they're—um, sick. You don't want to have them in there with your other animals."

It was a total guess that he would have other animals in the back, but it seemed likely. I crossed my fingers at my side.

"That's why they're at the sanctuary," Olivia piped up. "They have m-mange. It's incurable and contagious. Believe me, you do *not* want them in that van."

I shot her a glance. I couldn't believe my best friend sounded so calm. Only her flaming-red ears betrayed her tension.

Megan's eyes narrowed. "Mange? I didn't notice them shedding."

"It's not the shedding kind," Olivia said, taking a step forward. "It's rarer."

I realized my mouth was hanging open and shut it with a snap. In the distance, I could hear the faint wail of police sirens.

The man looked from Olivia to me as if trying to decide whether to believe us or not. The sirens were growing louder. He must have realized they were getting closer because suddenly he said, "You're lying," and ran around to the driver's side of the van.

"Police!" Megan screamed just as the cruisers roared into the parking lot, lights flashing.

"Stop! Police!" Officers leapt out of the cars, weapons drawn.

Olivia and I stood frozen, afraid to move. The last thing we needed was for the police to think *we* were the criminals.

"He has the otters in the back of his van!" I cried out, putting my hands in the air. I didn't want there to be any confusion over who the criminals were.

The officers closed in on Megan and her partner. One officer muscled the man onto the pavement and handcuffed him while another handcuffed Megan. A third swung open the doors of the van, just as Anson climbed out of another cruiser and joined us.

"You did it!" I squeezed his arm.

"*We* did it," he said.

I turned to Olivia. "Mange?" I said. "Where did you come up with that? I didn't know you were such a good liar."

Olivia grinned, her ears still red. "Just this once. Desperate circumstances and all."

"Mike, look at this!" one officer called to another. "This van is full of animals."

Anson, Olivia, and I walked over and peered in. My jaw dropped. The walls were lined with cages filled with snakes, turtles, chickens, rabbits—all fancy kinds I'd never seen before. Two empty cages sat with their doors ajar, waiting for our otters, no doubt.

"They're all stolen," I said softly. "They've all been taken from their homes."

The officer looked around as if he hadn't realized we were there. He smiled. "And they're all going back home, as soon as we can arrange it."

I smiled in reply. I'd never heard such beautiful words in all my life.

Epilogue

Once Megan was arrested, her confidence disappeared. She confessed almost immediately.

At the police station downtown, we all listened to her explain that she'd been stealing animals for the black-market exotic animal trade for years. Our otters—which she'd smuggled out of the sanctuary in her plastic storage bin—were just the latest victims. And they were indeed bound for wildlife cafés in Asia, just as we had suspected.

"I never meant for them to come to any harm," Megan said tearfully.

I didn't believe her, and clearly the police didn't either. The officer led her away.

Mom and Dad were shaken, I could tell, by how close our animals had come to disappearing forever. Not to mention how close Olivia, Anson, and I had come to dangerous criminals. I knew we were in for a lecture once things calmed down. But for now my parents settled for apologizing to Anson for suspecting him in the first place.

Back at the sanctuary that night, Olivia and I wandered down to the otter habitat. It was dusk, and the sun was throwing long, rosy rays over the ocean. In the cool shadows of the habitat, the otters were curled up under their logs, surrounded by leafy bushes, the lapping of their pool, the scents of dirt, ocean air, and growing things.

This is where they belong, I thought as we leaned on the wall. *Not trapped in a wire cage in a shipping container.* They were safe, and the people responsible for putting them in danger were going away for a long time.

Next to me, Olivia sighed happily, and I knew she was thinking the same thing: the otters were home.

About the Author

Emma Carlson Berne is the author of many books for children and young adults. She loves writing about history, plants and animals, outdoor adventures, and sports. Emma lives in Cincinnati, Ohio, with her husband and three little boys. When she's not writing, Emma likes to ride horses, hike, and read books to her sons.

About the Illustrator

Erwin Madrid grew up in San Jose, California, and earned his BFA in Illustration from the Academy of Art College in San Francisco. During his final semester, Erwin was hired by PDI/DreamWorks Animation, where he contributed production illustrations for *Shrek 2*. He later became a visual development artist for the Shrek franchise, the *Madagascar* sequel, and *Megamind*. He has designed cover art for children's books from Harper Collins, Random House, and Simon and Schuster. He currently lives in the Bay Area.

Glossary

contagious (kuhn-TEY-juhs)—able to be passed on by contact between individuals

exotic (ig-ZOT-ik)—introduced from another country

hysterical (hi-STER-uh-kuhl)—emotionally violent and uncontrollable

incurable (in-KYOOR-uh-buhl)—not capable of being cured

mange (meynj)—any of several contagious skin diseases of domestic animals and sometimes human beings that are marked especially by itching and loss of hair and are caused by tiny mites

trafficking (tra-fey-king)—to buy or sell something, especially illegally

vigorously (VIG-ur-uhss-lee)—to do something forcefully

Talk About It

1. All the adults in this story seem to judge Anson by the way he acts and dresses. Even Elsa judges him at first. How does Anson end up being different from the first impression Elsa has of him? Did your opinion of him change over the course of the story?

2. Elsa shows Anson how to help otters stand on their hind legs. Why is it important for otters do this while they are fed? What are some other things Seaside Sanctuary does for otters? Look back through the story to support your answer.

3. Elsa, Olivia, and Anson see pictures of animal cafés in Asia and Russia where exotic animals are kept so people can take pictures with them. Talk about some of the reasons cafés aren't safe for the animals.

Write About It

1. Megan works hard to make sure she isn't
    a suspect in the case of the stolen otters.
    Did you think she was involved as you were
    reading? Write down a list of clues that
    made Megan seem suspicious.

2. Pretend you're in Elsa's shoes. In your
    own words, write a note to convince your
    parents that Anson isn't responsible for the
    missing otters.

3. It's very important that the otters stay at
    Seaside Sanctuary. What are some reasons
    the sanctuary is the safest place for them?
    Write a list of reasons based on what you
    learned throughout this story.

More About Otters

Otters are some of the most playful and talkative animals. (Did you know giant otters can make 22 different noises?) Here are ten more facts that might surprise you:

1. There are thirteen species of otters. The smallest otter grows to about three feet (ninety centimeters) long. Sea otters weigh a lot more than river otters.

2. Otters have very thick fur. They can have up to a million hairs per square inch of their body!

3. While giant otters can make 22 different noises, baby otters have even more to let their parents know they need food or milk.

4. It takes a while for baby otters—or pups—to learn to swim; pups are afraid of getting into the water when they're first introduced to it. But once they get used to the water, it's tough for their mother to get them out!

5. River otters are great at swimming. They can stay underwater for up to eight minutes without coming up for air!

6. Most sea otters in the world live on the coast of Alaska. Others live in California, Washington, Japan, and Russia.

7. Sea otters hold hands while they're in the water. A mother will hold onto her pup's paw while they sleep so they don't float too far away from each other. They are also known to use kelp to wrap each other for the same effect.

8. Sea otters eat up to a quarter of their own body weight in food every day. Otters eat frogs, fish, crabs, birds, and more.

9. Humans are otters' biggest predator. Otters are sought after for their pelts.

10. Otters create tools from things they find around them that they can use to eat. Otters grab rocks to break open shells to get to their meal inside.

Seaside SANCTUARY

When twelve-year-old Elsa Roth's parents uproot their family and move them from Chicago, Illinois, to a seaside marine biology facility in Charleston, South Carolina, she expects to be lonely and bored. Little does she know that Seaside Sanctuary might just be the most interesting place she could have imagined. Whether she's exploring her new home, getting to know an amazing animal, or basking in the sun, Elsa realizes there's fun to be had—and mysteries to be solved—at Seaside Sanctuary.

Read all of Elsa's seaside adventures!

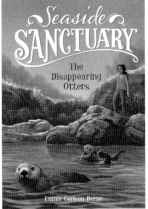

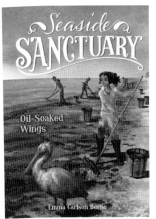

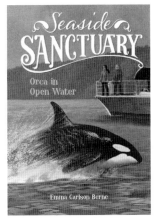

Use FactHound to find Internet sites related to this book.

Visit www.facthound.com
Just type in **9781496578600** and go.